The Sunbeam Path

D1512771

Nora liked slides and swings.

She liked colouring-in things.

She liked shiny red shoes
And jumping in puddles.
She liked bright blue socks
And she liked bursting bubbles.

She liked faerie stories
And loved story time,
And reading along
With Words that would rhyme...

The only thing better
Was when Rosie came by,
They'd blow bubbles outside,
And see whose would fly high.

"sssshusssssssh!"

Said Auntie Rosie
"They appear to very few...
Not everyone
Can see the world
Like little children do."

"These Wisps
Are not the faeries,
These appear only by day.
They're a smaller second-cousin,
The shyer Demifay."

4

Now Nora knew,
How rare faerie sightings could be.
She also knew that faeries
Prefer being called

"The Sidhe." *(The Sheee...)*

She hadn't heard about the Demifay before.
Of course her Auntie Rosie
knew a lot about folklore.

Rosie showed her how to glimpse them,
With a sidelong glance,
Because the Demifay would hide,
Given half-a-chance.

She showed Nora how
The Wisps could be seen,
Shimmering and shining,
In every sparkling thing.

Rosie taught her how
To use the crystal prism,
To create the sunbeam path,
And the colours with the glimmering.

The sun would strike the crystal,
Creating powerful blades of light,
And the sunbeam path would fracture
If the angles were just right.

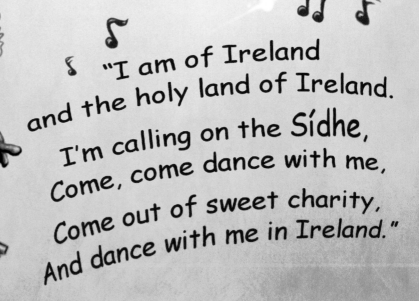

Rosie taught her a new song,
An ancient, magic verse
So the Demifay would hear her
And she could earn their trust.

"I am of Ireland
and the holy land of Ireland.
I'm calling on the Sídhe,
Come, come dance with me,
Come out of sweet charity,
And dance with me in Ireland."

Some Demifay

Wear cobweb shirts
Or flower petal dresses,

With complex spiral patterns
And silly, frilly tassels.

And long-toed, curly boots,
Or odd coloured shoes.

Some wear bits of shell
And have face tattoos as well.

Some Demifay have cool names,
Like Mauve and Heather,
And some of them look very strange
Like Coltsfoot and Feather.

Coltsfoot wears a cloak of green
As he hides among the grass.
He has spikey, yellow hair
And an arm ring, made of brass.

12

Mauve's skin is actually Mauve,
 Only mottled, like foxglove,
 Her hair is a turquoise blue,
 And her wings
 Have an indigo hue.

13

Feather looks
All round and blurry,
All soft and fuzzy
And very funny.

He Likes
The nickname Puff,
And bouncing around
Like a piece of fluff.

14

Heather is very fast
And fond of playing tricks.
She likes joining Nora
To practice gymnastics.

The Demifay love hiding,
In among the rocks and trees.
They sometimes use their magic,
Disappearing as they please.

15

Her brother teased her rotten:
Said they weren't really there,
Because he couldn't see them,
But Nora didn't care...

You never see germs either,
But still need to wash your hands.
You never see Sloths or Lemurs,
Because they come from other lands.

Nora would see them
By the river,
Or even in the bath.

Or would take the crystal prism,
And make
The sunbeam path.

A faerie lord called Caoilte
(Keel-Cha)
Appeared one afternoon.
He had a tiny fiddle with him
And played a lively tune.

Mauve told her how the faeries live,
In hollow hills or dúns,
And in enchanted castles,
Where we see only ruins.

She told her how Caoilte
Was of a different sort,
He rides with the faerie host
And has his own Dún or Fort!

Puff whispered secrets,
Of ways
From our world
Into their own

Of castles
And dolmen archways,
And magic circles made from stone.

Nora got very excited,
Asking, how could she get there?

When Puff suddenly panicked,
Crying "Oh you'd never dare?"
Mauve wouldn't tell her either,

Repeating:
"you're not allowed to know."

Then Caoilte, gave a flourish,
Saying,

"I can make it so!"

21

He said,
"It would be my pleasure
If you'd come visit my Dún.
The dolmen arch will open
In the light of the full moon."

22

And although she would have to wait awhile...
The moon was a tiny sliver,
When Nora told her halfling friends
They were all aquiver.

They were SO excited,
They jumped
And flipped
And twirled.

They couldn't wait until
She could share their world.

And meanwhile
They would visit,
Through the prism
And sunbeams...

And until she goes
To faerie-land,
Nora will visit
In her dreams.

Sweet Dreams

Readers Note:

The Demifay are generally shy creatures,
and while some people don't believe they exist
others only want to debate: how do you spell *'fairy'* correctly?

Should it be *Faerie* and *Demifay*,
or *Fairy* and *Fey*,
Demifaye, *Demifey* or even *Demifae?*

We believe that sometimes,
there is more than one right answer.

Coltsfoot, is well-travelled,
with a love for words.
He prefers the spelling *'Demifay'*.

Nora and Rosie let him choose.
They reckon he knows much more,
about Faerie Land, than they ever will.